go
girl

Music
Mad

hardie grant EGMONT

F
mca

Music Mad
first published in 2007
this edition published in 2012 by
Hardie Grant Egmont
Ground Floor, Building 1, 658 Church Street
Richmond, Victoria 3121, Australia
www.hardiegrantegmont.com.au

A CiP record for this title is available from the National Library of Australia

Text copyright © 2007 Rowan McAuley
Illustration and design copyright © 2012 Hardie Grant Egmont

Illustration by Aki Fukuoka
Design by Michelle Mackintosh
Text design and typesetting by Ektavo

Printed in Australia by Griffin Press, an Accredited ISO AS/NZS
14001:2004 Environmental Management System printer.

3 5 7 9 10 8 6 4

30827

Music Mad

by
Rowan McAuley

Illustrations by
Aki Fukuoka

hardie grant EGMONT

Chapter One

It was a warm day and the air conditioning in the car was broken. All the windows were down and a dusty wind blew everyone's hair into a tangle.

Iris didn't care one little bit. She was in the car on the way to her first music camp and nothing could put her in a bad mood. In the boot of the car, her saxophone was tuned and polished. She even had a brand new orange-and-purple sling for wearing around her neck while she played.

For four days and three nights she was going to be at Camp Melody. Imagine! Actually living with other kids who loved music as much as she did. Best of all, on the last day, they would perform in the concert – with their families watching.

'Iris?' called her mum from the driver's seat. 'Ask Kick if he needs to go to the toilet, would you? There's a service station up ahead, but we won't stop if we don't have to.'

Iris turned to her brother. He was reading a comic and had taken out his hearing aids because of the wind rushing through the car windows.

Iris tapped him on the arm. When he looked at her, she said, 'Mum says, do you need the toilet?'

He grinned. 'No, but I want a chocolate bar.'

'Hey, I heard that,' said their dad, looking up from reading the map.

Kick always spoke too loudly, even when he was trying to whisper.

'Dad heard that,' Iris repeated for him.

Kick shrugged. 'Well, I do!' He licked his lips. 'I want a huge chocolate bar with chocolate on the outside and chocolate fudge in the middle!'

'All right,' said their mum. 'I could do with some chocolate, too.'

'Mum says yes!' said Iris.

Kick threw both hands in the air and cheered. 'Cool!'

Somehow they got lost after the service station and ended up getting to Camp Melody almost an hour after the official sign-in time.

Iris stood by the car and looked over to the cabins. There were kids running everywhere, and a pillow fight had broken out on the lawn.

Iris's dad was unpacking her things from the boot when a young woman with very short hair and a clipboard walked over.

'Hello,' she said. 'You must be Iris? You're the last one to tick off my list! I'm Amber, your cabin leader.'

Iris suddenly felt shy and couldn't think of a thing to say. She wasn't sure what a cabin leader was, and that started her thinking about all the other things she didn't know. Like, where would she sleep? Would the other kids want to be friends with her? Most importantly, would they be better musicians than she was?

Iris felt goose pimples prickle over her skin.

What will the other kids be like?

Amber didn't seem to notice. 'Because you're a bit late,' Amber continued, 'all the rooms have been allocated. Don't worry, though. You're in with a really great group of girls. They were all here last year, so they can help you find your way around.'

Amber picked up Iris's saxophone case. 'Come on, I'll show you where you are sleeping.'

Iris turned around to pick up her backpack. Kick and her mum had wandered over to look at the river, but her dad was still with her. He had her pillow and sleeping bag.

'Let's go, kiddo,' he smiled.

Iris smiled back, but it felt a bit wonky on her face. She really, truly, absolutely wanted to be at music camp. But she also wanted to jump straight back in the car and yell, 'Step on it, Dad!'

Because no matter how much she wanted to be there, four days was a long time if she didn't fit in.

Chapter Two

Iris followed Amber across the grass to the cabins. Mobs of kids were running around, laughing, throwing balls and telling jokes. *They're probably all best friends from last year,* thought Iris. *I'm probably the only new one.*

The cabins were solid little wooden houses, each painted a different colour. Iris squared her shoulders and walked a bit faster to catch up with Amber. As she walked, she talked sternly to herself. *So what if you're the only new one? You'll only be new for today. By tomorrow, everyone will be the same. All you have to do is smile …*

She was still encouraging herself when Amber swung open the door to the red cabin. As the sunlight spilled inside, Iris saw three girls sitting on one of the top bunks. They all jumped with surprise. They looked like they had been interrupted in the middle of a secret meeting.

Iris's smile slipped a fraction. She didn't want her first meeting with her new bunk-mates to be spoiled by bad timing. Or by an embarrassing dad!

Just as she thought that, her dad pushed past her into the cabin and looked around brightly. 'Hello! This is cosy!' he boomed. 'Where shall I put your bags, chook?'

Iris grimaced. Chook! 'Just put them anywhere,' she muttered. 'I'll work it out later.'

But she needn't have worried. The three girls on the bunk were as great as Amber had promised. Instead of carrying on whispering, or giving her nasty looks for barging in, they were all smiling, waiting to meet her.

'Girls,' said Amber. 'This is Iris. Why don't you come down and help her unpack?'

Two of the girls climbed down the

ladder, but the third jumped over the side of the bunk and landed with a thud at Iris's feet.

'Hi,' she said, smiling broadly as she pushed her long fringe off her face. 'I'm Siri. I play viola.'

The other two came and stood beside Siri. One was tall, pale and shy-looking. The other girl had short dark-brown hair, and somehow Iris could tell that she was very kind.

'I'm Annabelle,' said the kind-looking one. 'I play violin. And this is Freya,' she said, pointing to the shy girl.

'Hi,' Freya said quietly. 'I play cello.'

Iris almost laughed with relief. It was

just like school! Siri was the loud, cheeky one, Freya was the shy and gentle one, and Annabelle was much like her best friend Zoe.

'I play sax,' said Iris, grinning.

'Oh, oh! Can I have a go, *please?*' begged Siri. 'I've always wanted to play sax!'

Iris did laugh then. She was going to fit in perfectly.

Chapter Three

'Well, Iris,' said her dad. 'It's time Mum and Kick and I got going. Will you come and say goodbye?'

Iris had almost forgotten her dad was standing there. She had been too busy checking out her bunk and letting Annabelle show her which shelves in the cupboard were hers.

'I'll come with you,' said Annabelle.

'Then I can show you the music rooms on the way back.'

Iris was pleased. It wouldn't feel like such a big deal watching her family drive off if she had someone with her.

Her mum and Kick were waiting by the car. Kick was practising his handstands, but kept tumbling over onto the grass.

Annabelle stood aside to let Iris hug her mum and dad. Annabelle pretended not to notice when Iris wiped away a tear while hugging her mum.

And then the car was pulling away and Kick was waving out the open window. Iris wouldn't see them again until the night of the concert.

'Come on,' said Annabelle, when the car had disappeared. 'I'll show you around.'

They walked together across the lawn towards the hall and the music rooms. A bell rang in the distance, and Iris saw kids running out of the cabins and towards the hall.

'Morning meeting!' said Annabelle. 'Let's go!'

Iris ran after her, leaping over the grass and feeling light and free.

Chapter Four

At morning meeting, Iris had her first chance to meet all the camp leaders and kids. It was a massive group and, as she sat down in the circle of chairs, Iris began to feel shy again. She looked across the room and saw Amber give her a wink.

A grey-haired lady stood up. 'Hello, and welcome to Camp Melody,' she said. 'My name, for all you newbies, is Libby. For all you old hands, welcome back! It's good to see you again. As usual, we are going to start off with a run-through of the camp rules and our schedule. Then we'll have morning tea. This is a chance for you to start working out who you would like to perform with at the concert.'

Iris felt jumping beans of excitement in her stomach.

'Remember,' Libby went on, 'your cabin leaders are also here as music tutors, so if you have any trouble finding a group, make sure you ask for help. Now, here are our leaders!'

Around the circle, each cabin leader stood up and said their name and which instruments they tutored. When it was Amber's turn, she said she'd have a go at almost anything except bagpipes. Everyone laughed, and Iris wondered what instrument Amber really played.

Then Libby posted up the camp program.

7.30   breakfast
8.30   music tutorial
10.30 morning tea
11.00 orchestra
1.00   lunch
2.00   activities (bushwalking, rock-climbing, canoeing, football, tennis, painting)
4.00   afternoon tea and free time until dinner
7.00   dinner

'Obviously, today is a bit different,' said Libby. 'To find the right people to perform with for the concert, you have to get to know each other. So, everybody up! Push your chairs back against the wall.'

There was a terrible screeching of chair legs on the wooden floor as the space was cleared.

'OK, everybody at this end of the hall – run! Now, run to the other end of the hall, but – *wait for it!* – only if you play *flute!*'

All the flute kids raced, pounding to the far end of the hall while the rest of the camp cheered.

'That's my group!' yelled Adam, the

woodwind tutor. 'Go, flutes! Go, flutes!'

'All right, let's see,' said Libby. 'Get ready to run and join them if you play *violin!*'

And so it went on, kids running and screaming from one end to the other, backwards and forwards. Kids who'd been playing for two years or less, then kids who played more than one instrument, then kids who'd been given their instrument by their brother or sister, then kids who were at camp for the first time …

Iris ran and ran, the group splitting and re-splitting in a hundred different ways until everyone was puffing and mixed together.

'OK!' said Libby at last. 'Well done! It's time for morning tea. I want you all to talk to someone new and start working out who you arc going to play with at the concert.'

Next to Iris, Annabelle danced with excitement. 'Come on, Iris!' she said.

'Let's find Siri and Freya. Siri's got a plan for the concert already.'

Iris figured that would be OK. After all, it was her first time at camp, so everyone was new to her, really. It wouldn't matter if she didn't make another new friend straight away, would it?

Iris and Annabelle found Siri and Freya under the fig tree by their cabin. Freya was sitting on one of the swings, while Siri swung so high on hers the chain went slack at the top of each swoop. When she saw Iris and Annabelle, she leapt out of her seat and sailed through the air, landing on the grass in front of them.

'There you are,' she said. 'Guess what?'

'What?' asked Annabelle.

'Tell them, Freya.'

Freya got up off her swing. 'I met another new girl at morning tea. Her name's Mia. She plays first violin *and* she sings *and* she said she'd like to play with us.'

'That's great!' said Annabelle.

Iris stood awkwardly while the other three talked. What about her? Did they have room for her to play, too?

Chapter Five

Iris wasn't sure what to say. Would it be rude to ask straight out if she could join in with the concert piece Siri had organised?

'Um, so what are you guys playing, anyway?' she asked.

Siri grinned and lowered her voice, checking over her shoulders as though someone might be hiding nearby, waiting to steal her idea.

'We're doing this folksong I learnt at school,' she said. 'It's great, because it's all for strings and voices, and that's exactly what we've got.'

Iris realised she was right. Siri played viola, Freya played cello, and Annabelle played second violin. And now they had Mia and her first violin. Perfect.

A perfect string quartet with no room for a big, noisy, brassy saxophone.

Annabelle saw her face and quickly said to Siri, 'What about Iris? Can we fit her in somehow?'

Siri glanced at Freya, and Freya bit her lip. They both looked uncomfortable. There was a long and horrible silence.

'Er, well ...' Siri was trying to talk, but she didn't seem to know what to say. 'The thing is, Iris,' she blurted out at last, 'we didn't know you when we started planning this. We really, really like you, but I don't think a sax will work.'

'But we're singing, too,' said Freya. 'Do you want to do the singing bit with us?'

'Yeah!' said Annabelle, turning to Iris. 'Can you sing?'

Iris pulled a face. 'Not really. Not properly. Only in the shower.'

'Oh, too bad,' said Annabelle sadly.

'Yeah, too bad,' Iris agreed.

She would have to find someone else to perform with. How would she do that?

After morning tea, it was time to meet up with the tutors. Some of the kids, like Siri, Freya and Annabelle, had already decided what they were going to work on for the concert. It was easy for them. They went off to find their tutors and pick out practice rooms.

Iris looked around for any other kids like her, who didn't know where to go or who to be with. She couldn't see any.

Why did I have to play the stupid sax? she grumbled to herself. *If only I played the flute or clarinet. Something normal ...*

She sat down on the grass next to her saxophone case. Inside, her sax was polished and shining, but what difference did it make how nicely it was tuned if she had no-one to play with?

She'd been so worried about getting stuck in a cabin with girls who didn't want to be friends, she hadn't thought to worry about the concert. Boy, had she got it backwards!

Chapter Six

Sitting on the ground, picking seed heads off the grass and flicking them at her sax, Iris sulked.

She wasn't usually a sulker, but today she thought she deserved some time-out to feel sorry for herself. She'd come to camp all by herself. She'd been brave and friendly and done her best to make friends. So why had she still ended up with no-one to play with?

'Iris?' said Amber, walking over from one of the practice rooms. 'What are you doing out here by yourself?'

Iris shrugged. She didn't want to make a big deal out of it, but she was sure Amber would feel bad for her when she knew that Iris had been left out.

'Why didn't you come and find me?' asked Amber. 'If you were having trouble you should have come to me at once. Now you've missed out on heaps of your first tutorial! Up you get.'

'But there's no-one for me to play with,' Iris protested. She was surprised that Amber didn't seem to understand that this wasn't her fault. She picked up her sax.

'No-one in your cabin, you mean. Or no-one you've met yet. There are heaps of other kids to play with, though.'

'Aren't they all already in groups?'

Amber gave her a lopsided smile. 'Luckily for you, no. In fact, I was on my way to find you because I have two kids still left over and trying to work out what they're going to do. I think you might be able to help each other out.'

Help out the left-overs? thought Iris. *I want to be in a proper group, not just stuck with a bunch of left-overs.*

But it was too late. Iris had wasted morning tea feeling disappointed and sulky, and now she was a left-over, too.

'After you,' said Amber, standing to one side of the practice room door so Iris could go in first.

Iris took a deep breath. Sitting inside,

looking glum, were two kids. Iris was surprised to see that they were both older. One was a girl with long hair, and the other was a boy with a pimple on the very end of his nose. They sat up straighter when they saw Amber.

'Here she is,' said Amber. 'This is Iris, here with her sax. Iris, this is Jess, who plays drum. And Caleb, who plays guitar.'

'Hi, Iris,' said Jess. She still looked unhappy, but at least she was trying to be nice. Unlike Caleb, who just scowled.

Iris swallowed hard. This didn't look good at all ...

'OK,' said Amber. 'I'll leave you to it for now. You guys talk about ideas for the concert. Tomorrow is our first proper tutorial where we'll start preparing the piece you've chosen. For now, have some fun getting to know each other and finding out what sort of music you'd like to play.'

They all nodded obediently, and then Amber was gone.

Have fun? thought Iris. *Not likely.*

She ought to make an effort, though. She was about to sit down next to Jess when Caleb started complaining.

'A sax?' he said. 'How's that going to work?' Without waiting for a reply, he went on. 'It's not going to work at all. Forget what Amber said. We might as well skip the concert altogether. No-one will notice if we don't play, and we can just spend the rest of the week practising by ourselves.'

'What?' gasped Iris.

It was bad enough being stuck with left-overs, but even the left-overs didn't want her! How dare they? There was no way she'd come to Camp Melody to miss out on the concert!

Chapter Seven

Before Iris could tell Caleb just exactly what she thought of his suggestion, Jess spoke up.

'Shut up, Caleb. Just because you're in a bad mood, there's no reason to take it out on Iris.'

'What?' Caleb looked surprised. 'I wasn't taking anything out on anyone! Sorry, Iris. Sax is cool and all, but let's face it, what can the three of us play together?'

Iris and Jess looked at each other.

'I mean, look at us,' Caleb continued. 'Iris, your sax is for jazz, and Jess, you've got an African drum. As for me, I've got a twelve-stringed classical guitar. I don't see what sort of music we could put together out of that.'

Iris struggled. She felt like throwing up her hands and saying, *I know! It's hopeless!* At the same time, though, she wanted to snap back at Caleb, *Don't be such a quitter! Of course we can do something.*

Except she couldn't think what, so it wasn't a very convincing thing to say.

Jess seemed to be having similar

thoughts. 'You might be right, Caleb, but shouldn't we at least try?'

Caleb sighed. 'Go on, then. We'll try. It won't be any good, of course, but we might as well do something to fill in the time ...'

Iris rolled her eyes.

Jess saw her and smiled. She rolled her eyes, too, and then the two of them almost got the giggles.

'Ahem!' said Iris, bending over to fiddle with her sax case so Caleb wouldn't see she was biting her lip to stop laughing.

Jess concentrated seriously on nothing at all out the music room window.

'Well, come on, you two,' said Caleb, in what Iris's mum would have called a *wounded soldier* voice. 'It's pointless, but let's make a start.'

It was too much. Iris and Jess burst out laughing, and once they started they couldn't stop. Jess was holding her stomach in agony, and Iris had tears in her eyes.

Caleb looked at them blankly. 'Oh, terrific,' he said, with a weary sigh. 'Now on top of everything else, it turns out you're both completely mental.'

At lunchtime, Iris met up again with Annabelle, Siri and Freya as they stood in line for hamburgers.

'We talked about every single piece of music we'd ever heard, and we still couldn't find anything we could play together!' she told them. 'And I mean really *nothing*. I don't know what we'll tell Amber tomorrow.'

'Oh, that's such hard luck,' said Annabelle kindly.

'Yeah, well …' said Iris. 'Anyway, how did you guys go?'

'Great!' said Siri. 'We've got Mel as our tutor, and she's tops, and Mia fits in perfectly.'

'Really?'

'Yeah, it's so funny because we all play at the same grade and she's even got the same type of violin as Annabelle. Plus her voice harmonises excellently with ours.'

'Oh, good,' said Iris, feeling a bit jealous.

'Are Jess and Caleb nice?' asked Annabelle.

Iris looked over to where Jess was eating

with some of the older girls. She spotted Caleb slouching at the back of the queue, obviously complaining about something to his friend, who was laughing.

'Yeah,' she sighed. 'They're nice.'

So far, everyone on camp had been nice, one way or the other (Caleb was the other!), but being nice wasn't going to be enough when they got on stage in three days.

Chapter Eight

After lunch, half the kids went bushwalking while the others went rock-climbing. Iris was in the bushwalking group, along with the rest of her cabin and Mia. They were fast becoming a gang.

'All right, you lot,' said Libby, who was leading the walk. 'Stay on the path and try not to fall too far behind. We're headed for the top of that hill over there.'

For a while, Iris was able to forget about the concert. She fell into step with the other girls and soon they were all puffing and laughing, tripping over the uneven track and telling music jokes.

'Hey, Annabelle,' said Mia. 'How do you keep your violin from getting stolen?'

'I don't know,' Annabelle smiled.

'Put it in a viola case.'

'Oh, ha, ha, very funny, I'm sure,' said Siri. 'Well, tell me, Mia, which is smaller — a violin or a viola?'

'A violin, of course,' said Mia.

'Ah, no. They're actually the same size, only the violinist's head is so much bigger.'

'Oooh!'

Iris laughed. The jokes were terrible, but bad jokes had always made her laugh, and Mia and Siri knew hundreds.

At the top of the hill, they stood and looked over the valley. Iris could see the red cabin she was staying in. It looked like a matchbox.

'We came a long way,' she said to Annabelle.

'I know, but we'll have to get back quickly now or we'll miss out on the good biscuits at afternoon tea.'

'Afternoon tea?' yelled Siri, overhearing them. 'Let's go, guys!'

Shrieking and whooping, they pelted back down the hill to the dinner hall.

Free time that afternoon was glorious. Iris felt like she'd been on camp with her new friends forever. Some of the kids were playing French cricket with a garbage can as the wicket, but Iris sneaked off with Annabelle and the others to a secret spot by the river that the girls had discovered the year before.

Just past the dinner hall, close enough to hear the dinner bell but far enough away to be quite on their own, they sat along the riverbank and told stories. They sat there and talked until the sun started to go down.

'It's getting chilly now,' said Iris.

'Yeah, and I've had six mozzie bites in the last five minutes,' said Annabelle.

'Me too,' said Freya. 'Let's go back before anyone looks for us and finds our secret spot.'

As they got up and brushed twigs and leaves off their numb bottoms, they heard the dinner bell ring. Siri yelped. Iris thought Siri must either be constantly hungry, or else she didn't believe there would be enough food for all of them.

'Run, guys! It's dinner time!'

They arrived at the hall in time to bags a table near the door. They all sat down, feeling pleased with themselves. And then Jess and Caleb walked in, looking around for Iris. Her heart sank. Just when she'd forgotten about the concert!

Jess spotted her and walked over.

'So, Iris, what are we going to tell Amber tomorrow?'

'Urgh, I don't know. It's like we haven't done our homework, isn't it?'

'Yeah, I know,' said Caleb. 'And we'll probably get into a lot of trouble.'

Iris and Jess rolled their eyes at each other.

'This must have happened before though, right?' asked Siri. 'They must have emergency back-up music or something, surely.'

'I hope so,' said Iris. 'I mean, I'm sure they do.'

Caleb sighed sorrowfully. 'We'll soon find out, one way or the other.'

Chapter Nine

Iris was so worried about her tutorial with Amber, she didn't sleep well. She kept having awful dreams about the concert. She dreamt she'd forgotten the music, or she'd forgotten how to play her sax. In the worst dream of all, she was on stage in her undies, trying to sing opera!

By morning, she was exhausted. She

felt like she hadn't slept at all. She hopped out of bed and got dressed while the other three slept.

Maybe if I go for a walk I'll suddenly get a brilliant idea for the concert, she thought.

Nope.

She walked around the camp until her sneakers were soaked through with dew, but she had no useful thoughts. She didn't have a watch on but it felt late so she headed back to the dinner hall.

At breakfast, she waved hello to Annabelle and the gang and then went over to Jess and Caleb. They were sitting together, and Jess was poking at her soggy cornflakes with a spoon.

'What are we going to do?' Jess wailed when she saw Iris. 'All I can think about is the fact that we have to tell Amber we don't have anything to play.'

'Me, too,' said Iris. 'I've been wracking my brains.'

Caleb was wolfing down scrambled eggs and toast. For the first time since Iris had met him, he seemed almost cheerful.

Typical, thought Iris. *He's probably happiest when things go wrong.*

At the front of the hall, Libby stood up and clapped her hands.

'Breakfast will be over in ten minutes. That gives you five to finish eating and five to clear the tables and bring your plates and bowls over to the kitchen. You then have two and a half minutes to brush your teeth and grab your instruments before tutorials. Your time starts – *now!*'

Iris, Jess and Caleb looked at each other. Twelve and a half minutes until they had to face Amber.

'So,' said Amber. 'What have you guys got to show me?'

Iris scrunched her eyes shut. Hopefully she'd wake up any second now …

'Nothing,' said Caleb bluntly. 'We've got nothing.'

'Girls?'

Iris and Jess shrugged.

'It's true,' said Jess. 'We talked and talked and really tried, but we can't think of anything we can play together.'

Iris waited for Amber to say something. To say she understood, perhaps. But Amber just folded her arms and waited.

'We really did try,' said Iris. 'But it's not easy, you know. We've all got tricky instruments …'

Amber raised an eyebrow. She didn't look like she felt sorry for them. She looked disappointed. 'Of course it's not easy,' she said. 'I never thought it would be. I did think, though, that kids imaginative enough to play unusual instruments would be able to come up with at least *one tune* to play for the concert.'

'We did our best,' Caleb protested.

'Did you? You really, truly tried your best, and you really think there's *nothing* you can play?'

Iris bit her lip. She *thought* that was right, but it sounded silly when Amber said it like that.

Amber went on. 'You couldn't even play *Twinkle, Twinkle, Little Star*?'

Caleb laughed. 'I guess we could do *that*, but we want to play something good, not some dumb baby tune.'

Amber breathed out through her nose. It wasn't exactly a snort, but it was very close. 'So what you really mean is there *is* music you could play together, but you'd rather sit around like lumps and not play anything unless you think the other kids will be impressed. Is that it?'

Iris blinked. Was Amber right?

'Well, yeah!' said Caleb. 'Of course we want to play something cool. Of course we don't want to look like losers in front of everyone!'

Amber gaped at him. 'Losers! What are you talking about? We're here to make music – what's that got to do with winning or losing? It's not a competition!

'And as you've brought up looking cool, Caleb, I have to say there's nothing cool about feeling sorry for yourselves.'

Iris gulped. Amber was right!

Amber sighed. 'Look, I know you

probably think I don't know what I'm talking about, but I do understand. When I was your age, everyone played flute. But what do you think I played?'

Aha! Now Iris would find out!

'Not the bagpipes, right?'

'Definitely not the bagpipes, but you are pretty close.'

'Trombone?'

'Banjo?'

'Ha! I wish!' laughed Amber. 'No, I had an accordion.'

'Ooh!' They all flinched in sympathy.

'Yeah,' Amber went on 'And you know what they say – what's the difference between an accordion and an onion?'

'What?'

'Nobody cries when you chop up an accordion.'

Iris laughed.

'Now,' said Amber. 'Let's get to work. We've got a concert to play in three days and no time to waste!'

Chapter Ten

It was amazing, Iris thought, how quickly things could turn around. At breakfast, she'd been feeling awful. Now it was morning tea, and she had never felt better. She hummed to herself in the queue for muffins and cordial,

'What are you humming?' asked a voice behind her.

'Oh, Annabelle! We just had the best tutorial! I'm so relieved!'

'So what are you going to play? You did end up with something, right?'

'Mmm,' Iris smiled. 'We're all set.'

'Go on – tell. Is it something I'd know?'

Iris laughed. 'Oh, yeah, you'd know it, but I'm not telling. You'll just have to wait and see.'

'I bet it's something cool, though?'

Iris smiled mysteriously. *Cool* wasn't quite the right word. In fact, it was quite likely that their performance was going to be the exact opposite of cool, but she wasn't worried about that anymore. Like Amber said, being cool wasn't everything.

The point was, she was going to make music. She was going to take something as ordinary as her breath and turn it into a sound that made other people want to dance or clap or cry or dream …

And that wasn't cool. That, if you thought about it, was amazing.

That afternoon, it was Iris and the gang's turn to go rock-climbing.

'No way!' shrieked Siri. 'What if I split a nail or get a blister? That would be a disaster for my playing!'

Mia jabbed her in the ribs with her elbow. 'Oh, don't worry, Siri. You know, if worst comes to worst, I know how to make my violin sound like a viola.'

'Really? And how's that?'

'I'll just sit at the back and not play.'

'Hey!' squeaked Siri. 'You think that's funny do you?' She chased Mia across the lawn.

It was another bright clear day. Iris smiled to herself and thought of Kick and her mum and dad.

I expected to miss them more, Iris thought. *I thought I'd have a good time, but I also thought I'd be homesick. I never guessed I'd like camp as much as this.*

'Oi! Iris!' yelled Siri. 'Are you coming or not?'

Iris blinked herself back into the world. The others were ahead of her, looking back and waiting.

Annabelle smiled warmly. 'She's just

daydreaming, Siri,' she said. 'You don't have to be so bossy.'

'Me? *Bossy?*' Siri pretended to be shocked. 'Iris, back me up. I'm not bossy, am I?'

'No, of course not,' laughed Iris, catching up. 'You're a shy little rose petal.'

'See?' Siri said to Annabelle, linking her arm through Iris's. 'Now, pull yourselves together, girls – it's time for a chorus line.'

One after the other, Annabelle, Freya and Mia linked their arms until all five girls were standing shoulder to shoulder.

'On the count of three,' said Siri. 'A-one, a-two, a-one two three – '

Everywhere we go-oh

People want to know-oh

Who we are-ah

And where we come from

And if they don't hear us

We shout a little louder!

And they high-kicked the rest of the way to the rock-climbing wall, yelling at the top of their voices. The song echoed across the valley.

Chapter Eleven

The rest of Camp Melody went by far too quickly. Time somehow sped up and plonked Iris down on the last day of camp.

In between the other music classes, everyone had been practising madly for the concert. Each day, fewer people lazed around on the grass at free time, and more of them went back to the practice rooms.

Jess and Caleb practised after dinner, too.

At their final rehearsal, Amber was encouraging them to relax with their music and have fun. 'Don't be so stressy,' she reminded them. 'It's not a contest. I'd rather you guys had a good time than get every single note absolutely perfect. I'd rather you played with some heart.'

Iris knew what Amber meant, but it was hard not to stress when you were performing in front of so many people. As Caleb had said, of *course* they wanted it to sound good!

But as they practised for the last time, Iris suddenly got it. If she got every single

note right, then the music would be perfect. But what if she made every note sing out with feeling?

If she could play like that, it would be better than perfect. It would be *magical*.

She felt her fingers move over the keys more lightly and easily than ever, and without noticing it, she began to sway with her playing. She imagined her sax was singing about sitting by the river with Annabelle and the gang, and watching Siri fly off the swing, and listening to Mia's jokes …

Before Iris knew it, Amber was on her feet and clapping wildly.

'You guys are awesome!' she cheered.

'Wow! I can't believe you're the same three kids who thought you couldn't make music together!'

Iris looked at Jess and Caleb. They smiled at each other shyly.

'Thanks, Amber,' said Iris. 'We couldn't have done it without you.'

'Are you crazy? I wouldn't have missed this for anything. And Iris, I have to say, that was above and beyond anything I've heard you play so far.'

Iris grinned. She couldn't wait to get on stage.

Gulp. Now that the time had come, Iris was feeling pretty nervous. She *always* felt nervous before a concert. She *knew* she always felt nervous, but somehow that never made it any better.

The little red cabin was a mess. Annabelle, Siri, Freya and Mia were all giggling with their own nerves as they got their costumes ready. Annabelle had brought four identical white shirts for them to wear, and Freya was tying lengths of gold ribbon around each girl's waist like a belt.

Iris looked up from where she was doing her hair in the mirror. 'You guys look great!' she said. 'Like a proper quartet, all matching.'

Annabelle smiled back. 'Your hair looks cool.'

Iris had braided her hair into tiny plaits, and was threading coloured beads onto the ends. When she moved her head, she could hear the beads clinking together gently. She had put on her concert outfit already – a pink shirt and her favourite jeans.

'Iris!' called a voice. It was Jess, standing by the cabin door. 'Are you ready?'

Iris looked over and saw that Jess was wearing a long blue dress and a chunky beaded necklace. Behind her, Caleb was wearing all black – black jeans, black T-shirt and old black sneakers.

She laughed. They looked just like their music! Nobody matched – they were all wearing different things in different colours, and yet somehow they sort of went together, too.

'I'm ready! Just let me grab my sax.'

There was no time for nerves now!

Chapter Twelve

On the way to the hall, Iris caught a glimpse of her parents and Kick getting out of their car, but then Jess and Caleb whisked her away backstage.

The dining hall had been cleared and filled with rows of chairs. A curtain was strung up at one end to hide all the performers between acts. Libby was making sure all the stage lights were working, and

Amber and some of the other tutors were handing out programs at the door.

Behind the curtain, the older kids kept hissing, 'Shh! Shh! The audience will hear you if you're too noisy!'

But they didn't have a hope. Half the kids were busy tuning up, and the other half were trying to talk loudly enough and fast enough to chase away their nerves.

Iris clenched her teeth and jiggled her legs. Jess and Caleb were going through the program to double-check where they were. As if they could forget – lucky last!

Annabelle, Siri, Freya and Mia were on first. They were standing closest to the curtain, ready to go on as soon as Libby gave them the signal. Iris wasn't sure what the signal was, but the hall suddenly went quiet.

The concert had begun!

Annabelle and the gang waited for their names to be announced and then walked out on stage. Iris saw them disappear through the curtain, and held her breath.

There was a long pause, and then Siri began to sing. A soft, skipping sort of tune. The others joined in, one by one, until all four of them were singing in a round. Then one by one, the instruments joined in, too.

Iris had never heard anything so beautiful. It was kind of sad and hopeful at the same time, with no beginning or end. Just one lovely circle of sound. Iris couldn't believe she'd been sleeping in the same room as these amazing girls!

When they finished, Iris clapped so hard her hands stung.

'Careful,' said Caleb. 'Don't want you to bruise your fingers until we've done our bit.'

Iris and Jess rolled their eyes at him and went on clapping.

Iris was standing backstage listening to a trumpet solo when Jess tugged on her sleeve. 'That was the second to last performance. We're next!'

They looked at each other and started jumping up and down, flapping their arms and wobbling their heads.

'What are you crazy girls up to now?' asked Caleb.

'Shaking out the nerves, of course,' Iris whispered back at him.

'Well, you can stop it right now. They're clapping, which means we'll be on stage in ten seconds.'

Iris and Jess stopped jumping and picked up their instruments.

'Our last act is a three-piece band, featuring saxophone, African drum and classical guitar,' they heard Libby announce. 'May I introduce … The Left-overs!'

Here goes, thought Iris.

The moment Iris stepped out from behind the curtain and into the light, her nerves vanished. She could hear the audience shuffling in their seats, but the bright stage lights meant she could only see Jess and Caleb. There were two chairs – one for Jess and one for Caleb. She would stand.

'Ready?' whispered Jess, setting her drum between her knees. She began tapping out a lolloping beat, like a rabbit hip-hopping across the lawn.

Iris tapped her foot along with it, and then Caleb started plucking out the melody on his guitar. There was a little pause, and then some laughter as the audience recognised the tune.

It was *Twinkle, Twinkle, Little Star*. But it was nothing like what anyone had heard before.

Jess hit her drum faster, and Caleb's delicate picking became a rock and roll strum, and then Iris closed her eyes and let her saxophone sing out over the top. The sax swooped and soared, and as it sang, Iris heard herself telling the audience about how three left-over kids had learned to fit together in a totally new way.

As they played, Iris wished it could last forever, but all too soon, it was over.

After the concert, there was a supper before everyone went home.

Iris's mum and dad pushed their way through the crowd, beaming and waving. 'Darling! You were incredible! I never knew you could play like that!' Iris's mum had tears in her eyes.

'I didn't either,' grinned Iris.

'Well done,' said her dad, giving her a crushing hug. 'I'm so proud of you.'

'Where's Kick?' Iris asked, looking around.

'Oh, he ran off to find your friend and try her drum.'

'Iris!'

Iris turned to see who had called her, and saw Amber edging sideways between groups of people. She had both hands high over her head, holding plates above the crowd.

'I brought you some cake,' she said, before she noticed Iris's parents. 'Hey, wasn't Iris something?'

'She sure was!'

'What sort of thing?' teased Iris.

'Well, what would the word be?' her dad teased back.

'Look, here's Kick. Let's ask him. Hey, Kick – how was your sister with her sax?'

Kick gave one of his hugest smiles and two thumbs up.

'*Cool!*' he yelled. 'Iris is totally cool!'

Iris laughed and laughed.

So much for worrying they'd look silly at the concert! Maybe music wasn't about winning or losing, or even being cool or not cool, but right now, Iris felt on top of the world!

Collect them all!

Sleep-over

Boy Friend?

Surf's Up

Sister Spirit

Dancing Queen

Flower Girl

Camp Chaos

Best Christmas Ever

Back to School

The Worst Gymnast

Sink or Swim

Music Mad

Class Captain

The New Girl

Karate Kicks

Secret's Out

www.gogirlhq.com